CAN YOU SPOT THESE STONE AGE INVENTIONS HIDDEN IN THIS BOOK?

Knives and scrapers

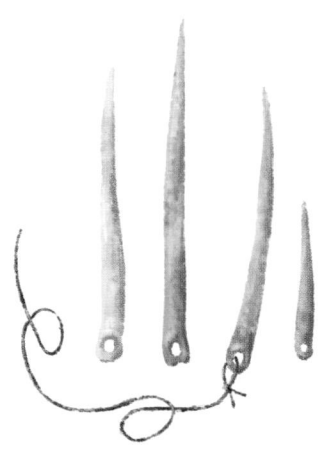

Sewing needles

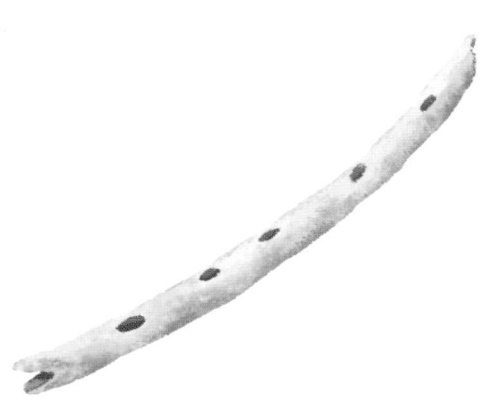

Stone Age flute

Lion man carving

Cave paintings

For Andrew, my own archaeologist.
CH

For Theodore and Nancy,
my little adventurers! xx
EE

SIMON & SCHUSTER

First published in Great Britain in 2021 by
Simon & Schuster UK Ltd
1st Floor, 222 Gray's Inn Road, London WC1X 8HB

Text copyright © 2021 Caryl Hart (www.carylhart.com)
Illustrations copyright © 2021 Edward Eaves

The right of Caryl Hart and Edward Eaves to be identified as the
author and illustrator of this work has been asserted by them in
accordance with the Copyright, Designs and Patents Act, 1988

A CIP catalogue record for this book is available from the British Library upon request

PB ISBN: 978-1-4711-8959-3   eBook ISBN: 978-1-4711-8960-9

Printed in China   10 9 8 7 6 5 4 3 2 1

The inclusion of author or illustrator website addresses in this book
does not constitute an endorsement by or an association with
Simon & Schuster UK Ltd of such sites or the content, products,
advertising or other materials presented on such sites.

HOW TO TRACK A
SABRE-TOOTHED TIGER

CARYL HART   ED EAVES

SIMON & SCHUSTER

London   New York   Sydney   Toronto   New Delhi

I love animals and I'm wondering what sort of pet to get, when a kitten appears in my garden.

"Here, kitty!" I call.

The kitten is just starting to come closer when . . .

"Albie!"

It's Mum.

"I thought your friend might like a drink," she says.

But the kitten is frightened and disappears under a bush.

Quickly, I crawl after it, pushing through the tangled branches.

"Here, kitty, kitty!" I call.

When I get out, a girl is holding the kitten in her arms.

"Is that your cat?" I ask.

"Yes!" says the girl. "He's called Claw and I'm Thorn. We're picking blackberries."

Blackberries?
YUM!

We are almost done when Claw wriggles
out of Thorn's arms and dashes away!

Oh no!

"Don't worry," I say.
"I'm sure he hasn't gone far."

Soon, Thorn spots some tracks in the mud.

"Perhaps he went this way," she says.

We follow the tracks down a grassy bank. But . . .

"Oh dear!"

"Oh DEER!"
giggles Thorn.
"That's funny!"

We search around for more footprints.

"What about these?" I say.

Thorn isn't sure.
"There's only one way to
find out," she says. But . . .

. . . It's a woolly rhinoceros!

"Quick!" cries Thorn.

"Follow me!"

She scrambles up a tree
and I climb up behind her!

"It's okay," says Thorn.
"We're safe up here."

SNOOORT!

She offers me a handful of blackberries.

"Might as well have our lunch while we wait!" she grins.

Eventually, the rhinoceros ambles away
and we slide carefully to the ground.

The next tracks we
spot are not right . . .

Nor the next . . .

. . . Or the next!

Thorn is worried. "If we don't find him soon, it will be dark!" she says. Suddenly, I hear a distant

Meeow!

"That's him!" I gasp.

"Come on!"

We follow the sound across a stream
and up some jagged rocks until . . .

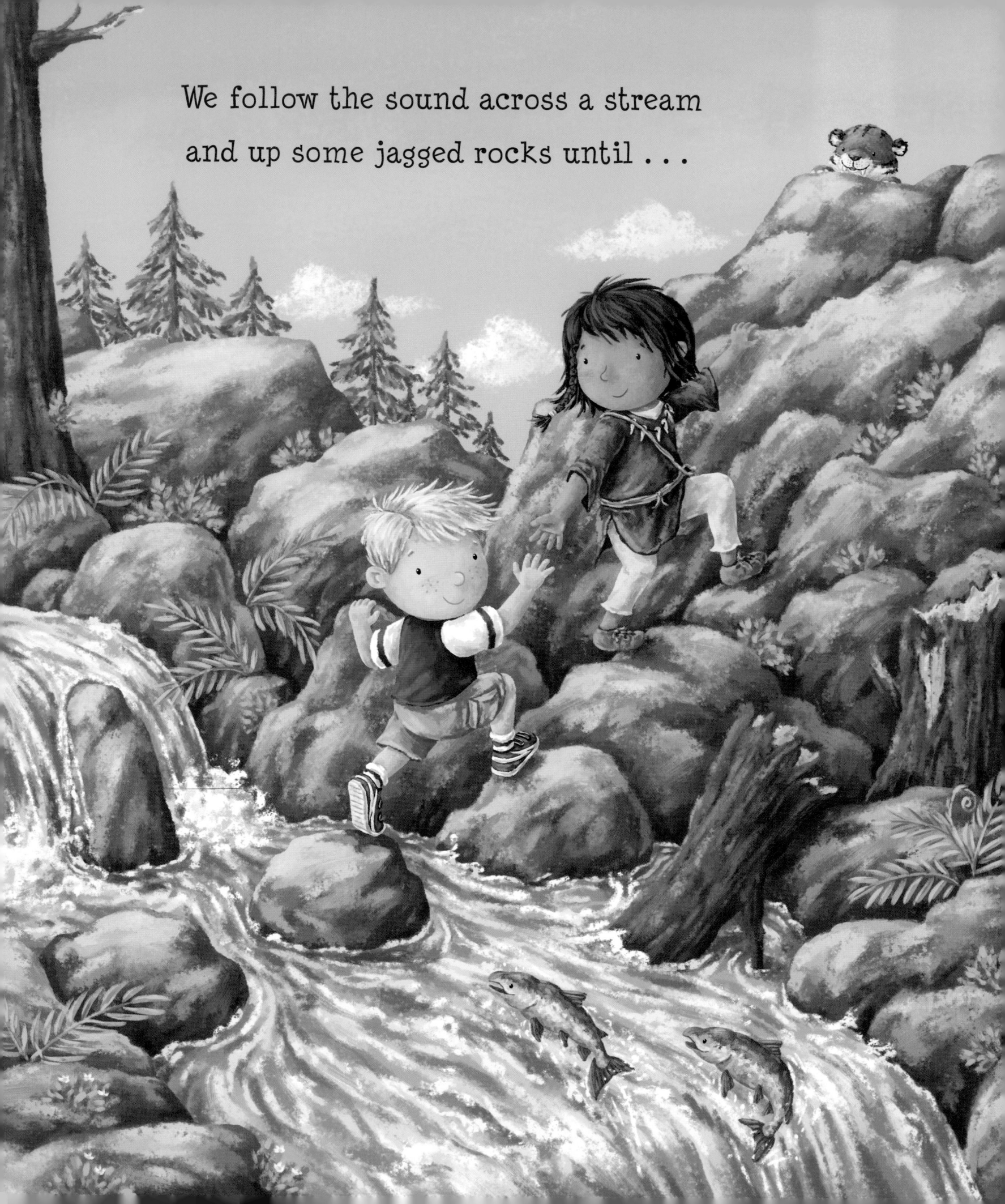

"There you are!"

Thorn scoops up the kitten and cuddles him close.

Suddenly . . .

I pull Thorn back and we hide behind a rock,
but Claw wriggles away and trots towards the tiger!

"Claw, stop!"
cries Thorn.

The tiger leaps towards him . . .

. . . and licks Claw
all over, purring loudly.

PHEW!

"It looks like Claw has found his mum!" I say.

Thorn sighs. "I suppose I'd better go
and find *my* mum too!" she says.

Thorn's home is VERY unusual.
We share out our berries and
then we paint our adventure –
straight onto the wall!

"My mum would go crazy if I did this at home!" I laugh.

"Don't forget to sign it," says Thorn.

Back in my garden, Mum is waiting.

"Sorry I scared your friend away,"
she says. "Perhaps it's time
you had a pet of your own."

Uh-oh!